LUMINARIES

LUMINARIES

KRISTIN KEANE

OMNIDAWN PUBLISHING

OAKLAND, CALIFORNIA

2021

Cover art & design: Katrina McHugh

Cover typeface: Avenir LT Std, Adobe Caslon Pro
Interior typeface: Adobe Caslon Pro

Cover and interior design by Cassandra Smith

Library of Congress Cataloging-in-Publication Data

Names: Keane, Kristin, 1981- author.
Title: Luminaries / Kristin Keane.
Description: Oakland, California : Omnidawn Publishing, 2021. | Summary:
"Agnes has been drifting away from herself. People look through her, her
husband doesn't understand her and lately, she's begun losing the sensations
in her body. When a tube of shoplifted lipstick awakens her back to life,
an impulse for stealing emerges that leads her to a court-ordered service
at a camp for grieving children. Hopeful the time there will help make the
stealing stop, when the spirits of the campers' parents realize Agnes can act as
a conduit to their children, she has to navigate using her compulsion to either
feed herself or help the bereaved. *Luminaries* is about the things we take and
the things that are taken from us. It asks what it means to exist in lives filled
with loss and to reach for the things we hope balm us-both in our material
lives and the ones we pass through."-- Provided by publisher.
Identifiers: LCCN 2021002388 | ISBN 9781632430939 (paperback)
Subjects: LCSH: Self-actualization (Psychology) in women--Fiction. |
Kleptomania--Fiction. | Grief--Fiction.
Classification: LCC PS3611.E164 L86 2021 | DDC 813/.6--dc23
LC record available at https://lccn.loc.gov/2021002388

Published by Omnidawn Publishing, Oakland, California
www.omnidawn.com   (510) 237-5472
10 9 8 7 6 5 4 3 2 1
ISBN: 978-1-63243-093-9

Here, they say *intubating tube.* They say *bedpan.*

Morphine. Anesthesia. Gunshot wound. The clients are seven, ten, thirteen. On the first day at camp, a boy named Crimson wrapped an invisible noose around his neck, pulled the rope and bowed his head toward his lap as if suddenly asleep. He was demonstrating for a girl with two braids tied at the ends in plastic knockers, what his mother had done to herself. Agnes saw in these children ghosts—souls fast-tracked into full beings within only a few years of life; they had lived two already—the one before the death, and the one after. *What will these children be like once they have grown? What will happen to their eyes?* Agnes didn't know death, but she did know what it was like to lose something, to feel like you were slowly blending in, disappearing from yourself.

Some of the children dress in costumes in the Exploration Lodge: a lion made from a headband of brown fur, a fireman, baseball umpires. Witches cast spells on professional chefs and dinosaurs—one spell for safety, another to end the curse of evolution. They are encouraged to find themselves, to act out when they feel like it. They are encouraged to become someone else entirely.

Yesterday the fireman's name was Christopher. He likes jokes.

"A sandwich walks into a bar. The barman says, 'Sorry, we don't serve food here.'" He is missing two front teeth, has a jack-o-lantern grin.

"Where did you learn that?" Agnes asked smiling, realizing immediately her mistake.

"My dad taught me," he said deadpan, before putting his leather helment on a nearby table and skulking away. Charlie, the lead therapist, watched from the doorway with his hands nestled inside his vest pockets. Later, he told Agnes she probably could have guessed by looking at him that Christopher's father was on late-night, that it was all over the news before she arrived. Agnes tried, but she couldn't make out the resemblance.

At the staff orientation, Agnes is told not to cry in front of the children, make them talk about anything uncomfortable, or engage in romantic relationships with the other adults at the camp. They sat on foldup chairs lined around the swimming pool at the center of the camp ground as the director Susanne rattled off additional guidelines. Agnes tried reading the messages the last group of children had written in spray paint on the exterior walls during a graffiti exercise but could only make out one in black lettering: *When will you be returning for me?*

The staff introduced her to the children as the summer's gardener because they couldn't introduce her as a thief—they didn't know about her court-ordered service, her purse full of watches and faux diamond broaches in the shapes of giraffes pocketed from the accessory counter of the local department store. She was a first-time offender. At her court hearing, the judge asked how she ended up there, whether or not she had a family. Agnes thought about Mark kicking the back tire of the car in the parking lot after picking her up at mall security, how he wouldn't look at her on the drive home. How he went to the court house with her that morning but waited on the bench outside because he couldn't bear watching his wife be sentenced for stealing costume jewelry. She shrugged her shoulders at the judge and adjusted the buttons on her black pantsuit.

"Not really," she muttered.

The stealing had come first as an impulse, like a knee against a reflex hammer: a roll of red lipstick in a slick gold tube she traced down its edge with the tip of her finger in the cosmetics section of the Rexall Drugstore. There was a moment when she could see herself in the packaging's reflection—her narrow face and shock of dark hair—the rest of her shapeless, no longer filled in, a wraith of what she once had been. For months she had begun disconnecting from herself like a balloon let go from where it was tied down. She didn't feel sad exactly but departed—drifting. Bus drivers looked past her; store clerks had begun looking through her. The sensations of her body's limbs and parts were deadening. She had taken to pinching herself at the loose skin of her thumb's base so often it was bruised into an azure spot that never shifted its shade.

She eased the tube inside her trouser pocket like it had always been there and then a surge pulsed through—

the aliveness that was missing. It wasn't a possession but a reckoning. A before and after that could not be returned.

Then: a roll of Scotch tape from the post office supply kiosk, a jar of raspberry jam stacked neatly on the glass counter of the bakery, a tin of chewing gum, a pack of batteries—each met with the same reward in the weeks of early summer when a menagerie of stolen goods began accumulating in a bag in the backyard tough-shed. Her mouth engorged with blood, the wrinkles at her lips filled in so much they glistened. She could see the pulse at her wrists, her veins forking off from one another like cyan tributaries. She thumped and hummed. She beat inside.

But when the security guard handcuffed her wrists together and left her sitting on a bench in the basement of the mall, the aliveness she had felt when the cashier's eyes met her handbag left her. She had gone too far and very suddenly wanted to stop.

The judge ordered two hundred and fifty hours of community service. Her parole officer fanned three brochures out on his desk like a tour-guide for criminals: months of slinging butter pads and two-day-old ham at the food bank, filing papers at the senior center during endless summer afternoons, or two weeks gardening at a summer camp for grieving children. Agnes liked the outdoors and she even knew some things about flora. She thought maybe the camp and the fresh air could light her insides again the same way the stealing had—could bring her farther away from the feeling that she was only getting thinner all the time, slowly slipping away from existence, colors that once had their own sheen, all smeared together into grey. Plus—a camp in the woods did little to entice taking. A camp was all tree trunks, sparkling lakes. Things she couldn't lift with her hands.

Mark wanted her to quit the stealing too. She knew it was something that had to die. While she filled out the paperwork, she considered how during all those months of tubes of lipstick and heavy pockets, some of the campers' parents had still been alive.

The set of cabins the children sleep in is called The Briar and the therapists work in rotating shifts throughout the night to help with crying and wet bed sheets. In the nearby Memory Forest, small ceramic wind chimes in the shapes of angels suspend from tree branches and clank together when the wind blows through. Agnes stayed in a cabin all her own, but during the first few days she took breaks from pulling weeds or tending to the things already planted, pregnant with life and ready to break open. She wandered through the play center where children gathered when they weren't attending group therapy. That day, most of them were at the lake surely trying to conjure reflections of their missing parents' faces in the water.

Agnes watched from a doorway as a boy named Henry pushed a wooden horse over to a small telephone booth in the playroom where he picked up the receiver. A small teddy bear in a plaid jacket was tucked into the pocket of his overalls.

"Howdy," he replied into the cordless plastic phone. His cheeks were ruddy, the color of cherry pits, blushed from pushing the horse across the carpeted floor. He talked to no one.

"Yes, ma'am. Yeah…Uh-huh…No, I'm doing okay… Nope, there's nobody here anymore except me and my trusty bear Watson… Stanley? I'm so sorry to tell you this, but he stopped breathing yesterday. Some kind of disease of the heart—goodbye!"

Henry put the phone down and turned to Agnes.

"You want to call anyone?" he asked, handing it to her before she could refuse. She thought of Mark at home without her, disappointed and ashamed, kicking the cabinet doors with the tips of his running shoes. Henry watched in anticipation, curling the plastic cord around his pointer finger like a pipe cleaner. She envied the way he could make it all up, how the sorrow on the other end of the line—the silence—didn't get in the way. He looked into her eyes and she looked into his.

"It's busy—," she said after a long pause of un-conjuring. She handed the earpiece back.

"That happens sometimes," he sighed.

Agnes saw Henry's ghost first. She laid awake belly up on her twin mattress later that night, the sheets as thin and stiff as an ice cream sandwich wrapper, a knot in a slat of the rustic wood ceiling just big enough to spot a daub of moonlight through. Closing one eye she pictured Mark on the other side of the hole lying on a bed of Hawaiian sand, his stomach burned red as lobster shells in the time before the stealing started, when she could still feel the way that ocean waves could tumble a body and emotion.

Suddenly the bathroom door creaked open all on its own. Agnes sat up, wondered if she had left the window ajar when a man came through in black trousers, his paisley tie undone at the ridge of his clavicle, excess belly spilling over his buckle. He was gasping but visibly transparent, his shirt and pants and face gossamer thin. She could see the outline of the dresser through his waist, and though she startled—a small terror against her stomach—she only said, "Hello," and pulled her knees up to her chest before he made his way to the end of the bed where he sat down wheezing, the give of the mattress bulging under his heft.

He started in about his heart right away which eased her nerves—the gambling and long lunches, the martinis with sidecars. The bearish stock market and too many cheeseburgers and his wife's affair.

"The heart can only bear so much," he said. The grey of his eyes glistened, and Agnes noticed the lines around them, the gold crucifix he wore at his neck, visible and shimmering against the shimmering skin where he'd unbuttoned the top of his dress shirt.

"I have a favor to ask," the man said, and Agnes

said yes because she had come here to feel more alive and he was sitting at the end of her bed with a broke-down heart and a hand resting on her leg.

He slid off the bed and stood next to where she sat so he could look into her eyes and she through his. He took her hand. She couldn't feel his, but she could feel the way her hand bent *in* to his, positioned as if she were readying herself for a mitten. He wasn't exactly as expected—the light around him wasn't white but orange, and he didn't glide the way she thought a ghost might but instead took steps like hers only they were soundless. His feet didn't crunch down on the beds of pine needles like hers.

There was no animus with this man-ghost with the tie and the gold crucifix. Every look he gave her was one filled with understanding. She had been slowly disappearing all this time, but *he* could see her.

He led her from Heart's Meadow where her cabin made a neat line with the other volunteers' and then through Memory Forest. For a moment Agnes thought that maybe this was all a dream until her bare foot came down on the ends of a desiccated tree stump and the zip of pain through her heel was so intense she fell to her knees. She had had dreams like this before—where her fear was muted like the rest of her, muffled underneath herself. But the wet slick of blood against her palm when she put her hand to the pad of her foot showed otherwise. This wasn't a dream—this was her in the night with a ghost.

At The Briar the man paused in front of door number three cupping his hand like he was holding binoculars to the window and signaled for her do the same. The stump of his finger aimed at Henry, a ribbon of golden hair across his small face, his arm hooked over his head ape-like as he laid in the bottom bunk covered in a patchwork quilt.

"My boy," he said, smiling, the creases at his eye filling up wet before pointing at the teddy bear that lay askance at the end of the bed, tumbled from a somnolent roll.

"Watson," he said. "I gave that to him as a birthday present." The stuffed animal had brown fur the color of walnuts. Agnes felt a tug inside herself, but she shook it from her body quickly as if it were a dusty rug.

The next day from the garden, Agnes watched the children lying nearby on yoga mats. Susanne led a meditation exercise and told them to picture their person and them in a quiet place together. Another counselor called Michelle walked by the mats sprinkling the children with water and bubbles like a kind of grief-priest.

During supper the evening before, Agnes watched how Charlie watched Michelle lick a smear of chocolate pudding from her mouth. The way her tongue intentionally lingered at her lips as she watched him watch, indicated Michelle was unaware of Charlie's children—the ones who drew hearts in the window of his wife's station wagon window when they dropped him off for employee orientation earlier that week. That maybe she didn't know that pudding was a lot like the department store watches Agnes had stolen—both rode the edge of changing a life's course.

"Where are you? How do you feel? Make your person talk," Susanne said.

Agnes thought of Mark in the kitchen the week after the arrest.

"Where have you gone, Agnes?" he had asked. "You're in front of me, but it's like you're not even here."

He had found the bag of stolen goods in the shed when he went to mow the lawn. How to explain the combination of items—the undone cellophane wrapping of so many things and the jars. How to explain the reason why they were shoved into the corner with the webs the spiders had abandoned. The day at the mall, she hadn't lied to him exactly, but she hadn't filled all the details in—how she was nursing a yearning long overdue. How the bag in the shed he didn't know about was getting filled up.

Susanne went on. "Now you say everything you've ever wanted to tell them, and hear everything from them you ever wanted to hear. Do this inside your head; no one else has to know."

That day in the kitchen with Mark, Agnes had told him she loved him—that it was worth it. That she had been trying yoga and jogging and anything else that summer to make her heartbeat drum against her insides to remind her she was alive. She had read self-help books and watched movies, but they weren't working. There was a block-up where somewhere there used to be a gush. The stealing had changed that. She knew he didn't want the truth blooming inside her since she had brought the lipstick home and drew onto her lips with it.

I'm alive, she had said into the vanity mirror, a circle

red as pomegranate seeds. *This is my mouth.* The things she stole gave her something. Cotton socks: the feeling of feet. A jar of nail polish: the sensation of fingernails. A charm bracelet: the concept of a wrist.

She gave in to salt shakers and bottles of aspirin and so many other things she could wrap her hands around and hold onto. She told him that sometimes someone can drift away but that she would do everything she could to come back, to be whole again. She hadn't yet noticed that he had been hiding something too—a stash of moving boxes collecting at the side of the house.

Agnes wanted Susanne to think she was still tending the lettuce and beanstalks nearby, but when she turned away from where she had fixed her eyes to a point on Crimson's baseball hat while she thought of Mark, she realized Susanne had been watching her the entire time.

She hoped her eyes didn't show the night before with the windchimes clanking, her hand around the ghost's. Back in the cabin the man had told her the truth—the dead can't haunt the living until someone gave them back a way to see. Before disappearing, he took her hand, kissed the ridge of her knuckles.

Afterwards she laid in bed. Being with the dead made

her feel alive, she thought. It was a kind of giving that was a good surrogate for the stealing.

A week into camp, Clementine asked Agnes if she knew that witches could change the weather and that spells could be cast for anything. She was a camper like so many of the rest of them who never got to say goodbye. Agnes showed the children how to decorate small patches of soil with pinwheels and bell tassels for their gone-person.

"You can make someone really sleepy or force apples to ripen." Clementine pulled three small stones from the center pocket of her corduroy overalls. "You can even cast spells to bring back the dead."

Agnes thought about Henry's ghost—about how she had seen that night the way the dead look at the living with longing, how the man watched his son from the other side. For three nights she waited, but he had not come back.

Earlier that day during a visioning exercise in the Exploration Lodge, Clementine whipped invisible eggs with a child-sized whisk, bringing the egg whites up into the air with dramatic effect. Agnes asked about the flavor.

"Chocolate," Clementine said.

"That's my favorite." Agnes dipped a finger in the pretend batter and exhaled with pleasure.

"It was hers too," Clementine said. "...Maybe if I leave it on the counter, someday she'll come back for it."

She has used the following words correctly in sentences: *melanoma, stage-four cancer, chemotherapy. Perished.*

Mark's favorite kind of cake was red velvet.

The stones were pink and shaped like apricots. Clementine explained each rocks' asset—fortune and good health—before pausing over the last.

"And that one?" Agnes asked, pointing to the third on the kitchen counter.

Clementine closed her eyes sagely. "It is for something so powerful, revealing its secret would compromise the magic."

During the bell tassel project, the children and volunteers were asked to discuss their fears. Agnes listed off all the things she was afraid of in her head: dying of ulcerative colitis, Mark being happier without her, elevators, ending up alone. Michelle sat across from her and Agnes wondered if she would make a big reveal—like how she was afraid she was violating all the therapists' rules with Charlie. When it was her turn around the circle though, Michelle held her to her heart and only said *spiders*. Clementine said bad spirits. Agnes settled on lipstick and all the children laughed.

That night something opened up in the knot of wood in Agnes' cabin ceiling though she never saw them come through it. The moon saw Agnes and Agnes saw the moon and the moon had been watching everything always.

A few more ghosts came: a professional dancer killed in a subway derail (red light for calamity), an anthropologist struck dead by a lightning streak in the Amazon (green light for natural disaster), a jogger run down by a circus caravan (red light, again). Yellow for homicide: a hole in the woman's forehead clean but wide enough for Agnes to look into and wonder what had once been on the other side.

Day by day more arrived for her. She led them to their children and pointed through windows or bush brambles, stood face to face with them, her eyes on their eyes; the ghosts' eyes on their children's. Agnes became whole again bit by bit, each spirit a gift bringing a need only she could fill. The dead were rehabilitating her as she gave them a way to see their children again, and the weight of the things she had stolen—the spoons and eggs of pantyhose, the pack of mechanical pencils, the handfuls of caramels and kitchen sponges—each fell off as the aliveness the ghosts gave her replaced the feelings all the taken things had once offered her. She was giving them their children back.

She wasn't even missing the stealing anymore.

Over the next week, the garden Agnes inherited came in. Beanstalks and pumpkins and heirloom tomatoes and watermelons swelled and lengthened under the summer sun. She pulled the rough stems from the ground, shook the dirt off, and showed the children how to harvest snap peas. At night, she showed the ghosts where their children had stood, the stalks they fingered and twisted from the earth.

"What are you doing with all your time?" Mark asked when Agnes called one afternoon, the ridges of her fingernails filled with soil. She was relieved when he answered since it meant he hadn't yet left with the boxes. She wanted *him* to offer an explanation before she told him she had found them. She wanted to hear him say that they were for a neighbor, or the holiday food drive, or for cardboard surplus. He didn't.

"I'm getting much better," she said.

"It's only been a week."

"Well, two—."

"Have you been spending a lot of time outdoors?" She thought about the way the ghosts held on—to her hand or her shoulder, the hem of her nightgown through Heart's Meadow. How the hues of their incandescent colors were like a rainbow of everything hard about living: sickness, tragedy, malevolence. The moon and the hole in her ceiling.

"Yes, you could say that. I've been helping a lot. I'm really helping things materialize, you could say."

Mark didn't respond. A moment later when she gripped the cord and decided to say she loved him, he was already gone; a hang-up without a goodbye. She wondered if she died right then what color her light would be—what color silence on the other end of a telephone might look like.

By the third week, the children's' ghosts began lining up with demands. They didn't just want an escort to see their children anymore, they needed a vessel: they wanted Agnes to get them their children's *things*. The first ghost came back for Henry's teddy bear Watson. Orange light sat in the same spot on her bed and explained how it was an easy fix, just in her reach. Hand in hand they walked through the Memory Forest to Henry's open window. Agnes put herself through the frame and took the teddy bear from where it rested at Henry's feet. When she handed the ghost the bear, he took it, his shimmering hands clutching Watson's faux leather belt at its waist. He kissed her again on the knuckles like he had that first night and took it towards the windchimes. He even smiled.

But before he disappeared into the dark, the rhythm came back. Agnes' insides became a kettledrum as soon as she had put her hands on the bear even though she didn't want them to: *this is a heart, this is a pulse, these are veins.*

Uh-oh, she thought.

Soon, others requested their children's odds and ends: a jar of multicolored marbles with slits like animal eyes, primrose colored sunbursts. A brush filled with hair entrails, a deck of playing cards, a rubberband ball. With these objects the ghosts could hold onto their children forever, they told her. They could conjure them afterwards *without* Agnes' help.

The first few were simple enough: she met the rush of

the take and it met her as usual. The ghosts told her secrets, took her hand into their not-hand and made her feel needed. It wore her down to think she was regressing, but it also raised her up—a strange counterbalance of stealing and giving and living and dying.

I'm still helping, Agnes told herself over and over. *I'm not even keeping these things for myself.*

There was no bag, no tough-shed. She was just a woman lighting the night with the colors of the dead, even though the tingle of her forehead wasn't the same. The sensations of her eyebrows had begun lacking feeling again. Taking things wasn't zipping across her body in the same way it had before the camp; it was deafening its edges, blunting its nerves. Stealing for the dead was killing the parts of her that she thought she had gotten back.

Clementine's ghost came to Agnes at the lake's edge beyond the Memory Forest, by the time it was too dark to see the golden twilight the volunteer brochure had promised. What light was left only illuminated a swirl of oil on the water, a dank mildew. The first pitch of a cricket cast itself into the air and Agnes pulled her knit sweater around her arms to steady against a damp fence post. A nest of flies circled a rotting lily pad.

There was a wrestle in a nearby collection of trees and then a hush. As she walked closer, she heard the laughter of a woman and then saw there between the branches, Michelle straddling Charlie, a corner of plaid blanket below her foot. Her shirt was undone as was his, a crescent of a breast-top revealed as she bent over to press her lips against his mouth. A dewy spider web connected two branches. Agnes knew if she didn't move, they would keep going but then her foot went too far, smashing itself against a rough leaf, the snap a firecracker. Charlie and Michelle shot out the other side of the circle running in separate directions away from her, the blanket left covered in bits of earth. The sun drifted out of the sky and all she saw through the spaces between the treetops were variant shades of sorbet smeared into a sunset.

Agnes pulled the branches apart from where she stood and came down onto her knees, laying on her back in the place on the blanket she had found them. She closed her eyes and tried imagining what it would feel like to have someone over her, pressing her down into the earth so that she couldn't drift away, but all she could think about were elevators and lipstick and Mark's cardboard boxes. But then, a new face came over her face in the opposite direction: purple light—cancer. A woman with sunken eyes, a bandana worn round her bald head. Her eyes lingered on Agnes'.

Hello, Agnes said.

It wasn't how anyone thought it would go, the woman explained—you can't haunt a person you love that much the way you hope you might. But touching their things made it feel like they were still with them. The woman said dreams changed when you died—it was hard to explain now, though, what exactly they were made of.

"Nothing ever new," she said. "No abstractions. Only clear memories on repeat-loops. Clear as day, every single one of them," she said. "No one ever tells you that until you're on the other side."

She wanted Clementine's stones.

"But she loves those rocks," Agnes said sitting upright, adjusting her eyes again to the dead. There were costs and there were benefits, the woman said. Agnes was her only chance. Agnes thought about the stones and there was a tug inside her, but it was the wrong kind: she had a thing going where she got to take *and* she got to give. The rocks were different. Clementine thought they were magic.

"I've lost everything," the woman said, opening her hands up to show the proof. "I have nothing anymore that I can love. I need a way back to her on my own."

Everyone knew Clementine kept the stones in the pocket of her overalls or sweatshirt—they were always easy for her to get to. The next morning, the woman followed Agnes to where the children searched for seashells painted primary colors. Hidden beneath rocks and leaves in a hundred square foot area of the Memory Forest, shells had words like, *Guilty Feelings*, *Jealous Moments*, *Strange Experiences*, *Happy Times*, written on them. The children collected them quickly by poking their feet around bushes, by getting down onto their elbows in a morbid kind of Easter egg hunt. Instead of opening plastic containers filled with jellybeans and quarters though, they fingered the edges of the shells and talked about what the words made them think about their missing person. One child's guilty feelings emerged because of relief—he didn't have to watch his father getting thinner anymore. Another had jealous moments when other girls' mothers picked them up from gymnastics. Happy times were hard to come by for all.

The children couldn't see the woman as she held Agnes' hand as the man had, gripping it tightly when she spotted her daughter Clementine prodding at a patch of soil with a long stick. The woman began crying, whispering her daughter's name—the roll of ghost-syllables as smooth and foamy as ridges on wave caps. The trees shook with each sputter. The woman put her hands to her face and a gust of wind upturned a nearby bench. Agnes looked at the ghost, but the children looked at *her*, standing alone watching them with the elements bending the atmosphere.

"I'm very sick," she said to Agnes. "I probably won't make it."

When the wind died down and the children looked away, Agnes responded under her breath, "How is *that* possible?"

"Ghosts die too," she said. "No one ever tells you that."

Agnes could see how the bend in her nose was just like Clementine's.

That day, Clementine wasn't wearing her overalls. The

purple unicorn-patched zip-up closed at her neck and then a flash of sunshine cut through the trees so brightly she had to shade her eyes with her hand. They waited at the perimeter of the circle while she undid the zipper, Agnes offering a halfhearted wave to Charlie who looked on perplexed as she stood by herself watching the children uncover the shells. Only, instead of dropping the sweatshirt onto the ground and running off with the other children, Clementine made a small nest from it at her feet and tucked herself inside. The woman looked at Agnes, and Agnes looked at the woman.

"Go to her," she said, and the trees shook.

Parting through the clusters of children with the woman trailing invisibly behind her, Agnes' foot accidentally uncovered *Lonely Times* lettered in yellow paint. She resisted the urge to pocket it, to take it back to her cabin and instead obscured the shell in moss and tree bark with the rubber tip of her tennis shoe before the children could see it. She approached Clementine carefully at the sweatshirt's edge. Her mother's ghost was there the whole time, watching. Agnes didn't want to, but she knew just how to get the job done.

"This patch of ground has a strange feeling to it,

doesn't it?" she began, leaning in close enough to Clementine to smell the dandelions clutched between her small fingers. She recalled the fear-circle days before.

"…Some say it's haunted by bad spirits, but—who knows? Have you seen the way the trees have been shaking?"

Clementine's body went rigid right then, but Agnes couldn't see her eyes. She couldn't bear to look into them.

"People say when the wind rustles the tree right in this patch, it's like they're trying to communicate with the living." She looked at the woman when she said this, right at her quivering chin. When the ghosts' tears came the maple leaves jangled like small bells. Clementine watched them.

"Maybe they're even here right now," Agnes pushed. "But *you're* not afraid of bad spirits—are you?"

It was Clementine the other children and Charlie watched as she fled, not Agnes. In the lining of the sweatshirt pocket Agnes found two stones instead of three, but took them anyway and placed them into the shimmering hands of her waiting mother.

Agnes walked to the pay phone that afternoon.
"I've tried calling you all week," Agnes told Mark.

She could hear the next door neighbor's dog barking at the fence through the line.

"I went for a drive," he said. "I had some thinking to do."

Agnes wanted to ask if the thinking was about her—how she was starting to get thinner again, how her hands and feet and wrists were changing, about her bag in the shed. *A five-day drive?* Agnes thought. Maybe Mark had his own ghosts—maybe he needed to stick his head out the window on the freeway and feel the way the elements blew against his body to remind himself he still had a face, hair, eyes.

"When I was there, I had a dream everything started vanishing," he said.

Agnes didn't ask if she was a part of the dream because he'd already started losing things too—himself, or her, or them—and *there*. Where was there, anymore?

He left it at that. She did not tell him about the stones.

She pinched the space at her thumb: nothing.

The taking went on, but it wore Agnes and the children down. Rumors spread between them and the counselors.

Each of the children made for a convincing suspect—they all had good reason to act out. Susanne brought the campers to a circle in the garden to talk about their feelings, about the things they missed. She looked very tired.

"Please," she said, "whoever is responsible—just make the stealing stop."

Agnes listened from where the volunteers stood nearby. In their parents' deaths, *things* only remained for the children—objects filled into the space their parents had left. *What consequence results from stealing from children who had already lost so much?* she wondered. She had tried to say no to the ghosts, but they rolled the ground or churned the pond water, their tears fat raindrops pouring through the slats in her ceiling making pools of water on the ground floor she had to capture with garden buckets.

They pled. In their deaths, a single object was all *they* had left of their children—a way to get to them again. Agnes wondered if the ghosts were there to help her become herself, or if they were a punishment for all she had already taken—the peppershakers, the watches, utensils, socks, the box of matches.

She had lost the feeling of her fingertips completely.

While Susanne went on, Agnes thought about what it meant to be a thief of grieving children when her eyes spotted the bush, the spot she had kicked the *Lonely Times* shell underneath.

Susanne had tried to inspire them to be in community with one another, but the children left the circle forlorn, missing their Barbies and stuffed animals, artifacts their parents left imprinted on them. Agnes was the only one who left with something tangible: an idea materialized on that patch of dirt; a born-thing.

She was not as compliant when the next ghost came.

"What are you going to do for *me*?" she asked the ballerina, who stood with her right severed leg tucked under her arm for counterbalance. She wore small pearl earrings and drawstring pants, her chiseled shoulders were dusted with gold freckles.

"I'm dead," she said with a shrug. She wanted her daughter Elizabeth's watch.

"You need to leave something for me to give to her," Agnes said, "…—or else, I'm not going to do it."

The ballerina explained how the dead have nothing;

she *needed* that leg, if that's what Agnes was suggesting—*and* she needed the watch.

"Not your *leg*—," Agnes says, "A message. Give me a note to leave in its place so she'll know it was you."

The ballerina's eyebrows knitted together and for a moment Agnes could see the kind of mother she had been—measured, patient, intentional.

"We had this saying in our family to explain difficult circumstances: *Truth is stranger than fiction*, is what we'd say. Tell her that. She'll know it's from me."

After Agnes found Elizabeth's watch in the locker room where she discarded it before leaving for the swimming pool, she gave it to the ballerina and went straight to the garden to the patch under the bush. With a small paintbrush in hand, she went to work on the seashell.

Agnes did not tend the garden the last week, and the sunbaked runner beans secured to trellises withered into shriveled finger-lengths under the hot sun. The carrots did the same—tentacles spilled onto the ground covering it in a limp green wig. The peppers frazzled hard as leather near a series of pumpkins sunk in on themselves like deflated basketballs. All that Agnes made was dying, but with a few days left of camp she was building something that stealing or ghosts could not take away.

Blue light: infection. A jaundiced mailman with a bloody dog bite across his right shin. He gave Agnes, *You're as beautiful as your mother*, for a set of baseball cards.

Red light: car accident. Two collapsed lungs, a dentist's chest sunk in like a punctured soufflé. She asked for a pair of socks in exchange for, *To the moon and back*.

Grey: suicide. A romance novelist wanted her daughters heart-shaped photo album. She gave Agnes, *Don't let the bastards grind you down*.

Agnes did this night by night, ghost by ghost, message by message.

Each day Agnes called home, but she couldn't get an answer on the other end. For ten minutes at a time she held the line depositing one quarter after the next, trying to conjure the ringing into a forgiveness, trying to summon her inner ear from the vibrations of the handset. She told herself, *This is my cartilage. This is my eustachian tube.* Agnes tried picturing Mark in the kitchen, the hallway, their bedroom, but all she could think of were the boxes, his empty dresser drawers and how he'd collected far too many to fill. She had counted them just weeks ago when she had found them at the side of the house—the morning she left for camp. For all those months she'd been taking, he'd been collecting. He was planning to leave before he even knew about the stealing. One box probably just for his favorite sweater, another dedicated to paperclips.

Agnes kept working. She kept collecting messages. She tried to feel her pulse.

The last night at camp was a celebration, the theme: *Future.* The children painted welcome signs onto butcher paper for the leftover family who would return for them the next morning. Each sign said what they looked forward to when they went home—little blobs of paint dripping down like tears. This was an exercise in tunnel vision, a way of shunting the obvious: no thing could ever replace what they missed most. The idea of looking forward to something had been stripped from each of their hands well before they arrived at camp. Agnes thought about her bag of shed goods, if by then there was actually anything left in the shed or at home at all.

She got stationed at the fortune teller booth. It was hard to incorporate vegetables and fruits into a motif about future-time especially since they all had regressed, especially since she had let each alive thing slip into their slow discolored cantaloupe deaths. Susanne gave her an orbuculum and a scarf which she tied at her waist.

Crimson was her only customer, standing at the booth while Agnes looked into the orb. She started in about the crystal ball—how it could unlock all the secrets of what was to come. She said things she had heard on television shows and infomercials.

"What color is it? What color is it in your magic ball?" Crimson asked. Agnes thought about red, purple, green, yellow—how each tone bore a particular kind of sadness, then a woman slid through the trees and stood beside her son.

"Take his baseball cap off his head," she instructed Agnes. Side by side she could see he had her hairline. Her strong jaw.

Crimson's hat was a worn out blue; two embroidered dolphins bent into a heart above the bill.

Agnes said, "Don't be ridiculous—," and the boy's

mouth turned down. "Not *you*!" She waved her arms back and forth to suggest the magic of the future and signal the ghost to move away.

"But I *need* that cap—," the woman pled from her grey glow, her chest a sunken ship. "...It was his father's favorite too... He was a boatman." Every word was a wheeze, air slipping from a bike tire's hole.

Was. Agnes remembered Crimson's make-believe noose and it all folded together.

Smiling at the boy, she tried ignoring the ghost who went on with her reasons—how she thought in dying she might be able to find her husband; how she thought if there was a heaven, she could sail with him on a heavenly sea. Agnes tried offering the boy a fortune, a fraudulent vision. She asked him to imagine a quiet place, a beach. The boy closed his eyes while the spirit of his mother kept up, the breath of her gasps rattling the booth, stirring the leaves on the ground.

"Make sand," Agnes directed. "Make a wave." She got louder to best the ghost, and the other nearby children paused to watch the pine cones and dirt churn into twisters at their feet. Agnes noted how they were picking up steam, how frustrated the ghost was becoming. She tried a compromise.

"Is your mother there on the beach with you?" Agnes shouted at Crimson, watching the ghost watch the boy open his eyes to watch Agnes.

"Yes—!"

"Is she the sunshine?"

"No," he said.

"Is she the tide at the sand's edge?"

"No," he insisted.

"Is she the wave?"

"*No*—," Crimson said, "—but the wave is really important." He looked at Agnes. "It's carrying her and my father back to me in a cola bottle."

Agnes stopped. She looked at his head and the swirling and the wind.

"Tell me something: does the wave want you to give up your hat?"

Before the ghost could respond or Agnes could respond or the boy could respond, shouting from the swimming pool quieted the screaming wind.

Charlie found him first, face down in the swimming

pool, his windbreaker puffed out around him like a nylon parachute. Christopher floated in the center of the water, the long tubes of the vacuum hose twisting around the nearby leaf-catch, his body illuminated by the submersible lights under the water line.

"Oh god," Agnes said standing in her waisted scarf, unable to hear herself over the screaming as the other staff stampeded to ring the perimeter of the pool.

Charlie dove straight in and reached to turn Christopher onto his back. Susanne looked across the patio at Agnes, her face flushed and panicked. Michelle crouched down at the pool's edge. Someone else stepped into the water and waited.

Charlie held him like a baby when he emerged from the shallow end—jeans waterlogged and sagging at the waist. When he laid Christopher on the wet concrete, two others leaned over his small body, obscuring his face before retracting very suddenly when the boy sat up, his wet hair pasted to his head like a swimming cap. He took heaving breaths and then grinned.

There in the center of the adults, his fellow campers,

he began clapping for himself—a faked death, a grand joke. It was a singular applause in an audience of horror. Across the corridor, Susanne swallowed a sob before running to the bathroom.

"Do you believe in magic?" Susanne asked Agnes after she followed her inside. Her eyes were smeared with black mascara and bits of toilet paper stuck to the places where she dabbed at her tears. Agnes sat on the turned down lid of a toilet.

Agnes didn't answer, but Susanne went on anyway. "At night I pray for something to make all of this," she waved her hands around in a circle above her head, "...just go away."

Agnes wasn't sure if she meant her thoughts, or the camp, or what brought them all there together, or even if she meant *her*, but she decided not to ask. Instead, she went to Susanne and put two fingers to the wet streak of make-up and tears on her cheek, and as if her fingers were paintbrushes, drew two circles around her own eyes with them.

Later, after dinner the children cast lanterns into the

night sky as planned. Christopher skulked by a tree. They decorated the onion-skin paper with notes to their parents and sent them up during a lighting ceremony led by Charlie. His clothes still dripped with pool water.

I want you to know I will do a good job.

I will never forget you.

Please come back to me soon.

No one will ever take your place.

I can't stop missing you.

The volunteers also took turns. Agnes thought of Mark, how he used to rub her ears until she fell asleep at night.

I'll stop—she wrote. She added a caret. *I'll try to stop*, it read. She cast the lantern away from herself.

She walked back to her cabin and looked through the hole in the ceiling. She couldn't feel her back or her neck or her legs. She couldn't see the moon.

No ghosts came.

In the morning, the therapists and volunteers lined the children up before taking them to the Memory Forest for a goodbye circle. The staff had been quiet and uneasy since the scene at the pool, and Charlie and Michelle allowed for a healthy distance. There were no more lingering glances, no intentional brush-ups since the night before.

"What does the early bird get?" Christopher asked Agnes, and it was then she could finally see the family resemblance—the curled red hair, the shape of his eyebrows, even the way he turned his head to the side before hitting the punch line just the way his father did on television. He told Susanne he had practiced holding his breath at night since the first day he noticed the swimming pool, timing himself in his cabin after lights-out. The staff met to discuss it, but no one could come up with a consequence for a boy who came to mourn his father, the stand-up comic.

"The worm?" Agnes responded.

"Yes—and what about the late bird? What does it get?"

"I'm not sure," she said.

He paused for a moment the way he had been trained to do, to build the suspense.

"The late bird is the one who gets to live," he said without smiling. He stepped away.

Clementine came next and took Agnes by the wrist,

put a stone into the palm of her hand.

"The others are gone, but I had been saving the third one for you," Clementine said, pressing her fingers down onto the rock. Agnes couldn't feel its rough contours even though she could see them. "It's to cure heartbreaks." She held it there for a moment before Agnes pulled away. She was relieved Clementine would never know—she wouldn't have to watch her mother die again.

Agnes slipped away from the line-up. She passed the languishing garden green, ends and stalks singed by the heat. She passed the angel chimes. Her cabin. *This is my breath*, she thought though she couldn't feel it.

In the Memory Forest she had made a circle with all the seashells she painted over where they would all gather before leaving—one for each child, from their ghost. She had erased the feelings—the guilt and the joy, the jealousy and despair—and instead left the words of their parents so the children would know their things were taken with great purpose; that a message had come over the line. *You'll get older, but you'll get wiser. Never bet against the house. All you can ever do is your best.* The shells were the color of tragedy: cancer, accidents, cardiac arrest. The messages were some kind of hope.

At the fire pit she took off her clothes and washed her hands with the soot and earth left behind by three weeks of smoldering log rolls and crumpled newspaper. She dragged her hands down the mossy sides of a nearby tree, painted the spaces between her fingers with their green pulp.

This is my breath this is my breath this is my breath.

She drew her hands up each arm, marked them with the ash. *These are my bones. This is skin.* From there, her hands ran across her chest, the space at her cleavage. *These are ribs. This is tissue, fat. A breast plate*, she thought.

Down her stomach, the convex shape of her inner thighs. Knees, femur, feet, arches. She took her own face in her hands and outlined her nose, her mouth, her eye sockets with the end of a burnt chip of bark.

She kept walking.

This is my breath this is my breath this is my breath.

At Heart's Meadow, Agnes vanished into the trees.

Kristin Keane's work has appeared with the *New England Review*, *The Normal School*, *Electric Literature* and elsewhere. She lives in San Francisco. More of her work can be found at thisisnotreallyhere.space.

Luminaries
by Kristin Keane

Cover art & design: Katrina McHugh

Cover typeface: Avenir LT Std, Adobe Caslon Pro
Interior typeface: Adobe Caslon Pro

Cover and interior layout by Cassandra Smith

Printed in the United States
by Books International, Dulles, Virginia
On 55# Glatfelter B19 Antique
Acid Free Archival Quality Recycled Paper

Publication of this book was made possible in part by gifts from
Katherine & John Gravendyk in honor of Hillary Gravendyk,
Francesca Bell, Mary Mackey, and The New Place Fund

Omnidawn Publishing
Oakland, California
Staff and Volunteers, Spring 2021

Rusty Morrison & Ken Keegan, senior editors & co-publishers
Kayla Ellenbecker, production editor & poetry editor
Gillian Olivia Blythe Hamel, senior editor & book designer
Trisha Peck, senior editor & book designer
Rob Hendricks, Omniverse editor, marketing editor & post-pub editor
Cassandra Smith, poetry editor & book designer
Sharon Zetter, poetry editor & book designer
Liza Flum, poetry editor
Matthew Bowie, poetry editor
Anthony Cody, poetry editor
Jason Bayani, poetry editor
Juliana Paslay, fiction editor
Gail Aronson, fiction editor
Izabella Santana, fiction editor & marketing assistant
Laura Joakimson, marketing assistant specializing in Instagram & Facebook
Ashley Pattison-Scott, executive assistant & Omniverse writer
Ariana Nevarez, marketing assistant & Omniveres writer